JAMES PRELLER

ONE-EYED DOLL

SCARY TALES

Illustrated by IACOPO BRUNO

FEIWEL AND FRIENDS
New York

A FEIWEL AND FRIENDS BOOK
An Imprint of Macmillan

Feiwel and Friends books may be purchased for business or promotional
use. For information on bulk purchases, please contact the Macmillan
Corporate and Premium Sales Department at (800) 221-7945 x5442 or by
e-mail at specialmarkets@macmillan.com.

Library of Congress Cataloging-in-Publication Data Available

ISBN: 978-1-250-04094-7 (hardcover) / 978-1-250-04095-4 (paperback)
978-1-250-06422-6 (ebook)

Book design by Ashley Halsey

Feiwel and Friends logo designed by Filomena Tuosto

First Edition: 2014

10 9 8 7 6 5 4 3 2 1

mackids.com

This book is dedicated to the memory of Rod Serling,
creator of The Twilight Zone *TV series.*

CONTENTS

COME
CLOSER . . .

SHE WON'T...

BITE.

ONE DAY YOU MIGHT FIND A BOX, JUST LIKE THE CHILDREN IN THIS STORY. MAYBE YOU AND YOUR FRIENDS WILL DIG IT UP. THERE MIGHT BE A LOCK ON IT.

AND YOU'LL WONDER . . . "WHAT'S INSIDE?"

MAYBE IT'S SOMETHING GREAT. TREASURE, RICHES, FORTUNE.

COME ON, WHY WAIT?

WHAT COULD POSSIBLY GO WRONG?

MALIK AND TIANA

The Rice children, Malik and Tiana, often played Treasure Hunt together—especially during the oven-hot days of summer. They had never discovered any actual treasure, but that didn't stop them from trying. Some days they found golf balls, weird rocks, old bottles. Mostly the hunt was just an excuse to wander under the cool umbrella of the dark woods. It was, they agreed, a good way to kill the blistering, hot days.

Besides, you never know. As Malik said, "We're not gonna find treasure, Tiana, if we never go looking for it."

Malik was ten years old. He was "the responsible one." The serious one. Good teeth, clean hands. The boy who could be trusted to look after his little sister, wild Tiana, and keep her from harm.

Malik didn't mind. Not much, anyway. He might even tell you that he loved his sister's wild black curls, her thin muscular arms, the way she seemed to float across rooms in yellow dresses. On some days, of course, Malik would frown and darken his gaze. It was hard to *always* be the responsible one. Like a weight he carried on his shoulders, day after day.

"No, Tiana, get off that ledge."

"Put that down, Tiana. That's glass."

"Not now, Tiana, Daddy's sleeping. Leave him be."

Their father, Mr. Charles Rice, worked nights at the factory. Malik never figured out what exactly his Daddy did there, except that he returned home bone-tired and ready for bed. Right about the time most folks were getting up! Because of that simple fact—"Papa needs his sleep"—there was much tiptoeing around the house. Mama always said things like, "Shush, children," and "Quiet now, Papa's sleeping." School days, it wasn't too bad. Off on the bus they'd go, **CLACKETY-CLACK**, and away they went. But in the summer when Malik and Tiana were footloose and free, the house felt like a musty old library. *Hush now, children, don't say a word*. Malik figured it was best to get outdoors and greet the day.

Most mornings, Mama went off to her job (Mama worked in the kitchen at the "old age" home). Everybody in the Rice family had a job, she said, even Malik and Tiana.

Malik's job was looking after his free-spirited sister. Tiana's job? Nobody had quite figured that out. She smiled and laughed, twinkled and danced. Maybe that was her role after all, just to shine like the sun. Tiana was a happy soul, so maybe making folks happy was her task in life. She lit up rooms like a 100-watt bulb. She laughed and the world laughed with her.

One bad day, Tiana wandered over to the old place. That was the name of it, exactly that: *the old place*. Ask anybody in the neighborhood, they'd all know the spot you were talking about. The old, abandoned house at the edge of the woods. It was a falling-down, battered old place that had been empty for years. A real eyesore, everybody called it. One shudder swung loose on a nail—*bang, bang, bang*—and slammed against the house like a warning in the wind. Haunted, maybe.

Nobody remembered folks ever living there, or if they did recall it, they didn't say so. Except to repeat, "Now, you kids, stay away from that old place."

That was the warning heard up and down the block.

STAY AWAY FROM THAT OLD PLACE.

"Why?" the children sometimes asked.

And the answer was always the same, "Nothing good can come of it, that's all. Just stay away. Understand?"

Malik and Tiana nodded their heads.

They understood.

At least, one of them did.

The other one wasn't as good at listening.

TIANA GOES MISSING

On this particular afternoon, Malik and Tiana were joined by their neighbor, Soda Pop.

Soda Pop was not his real name, of course. It says Arthur on his birth certificate. But somewhere along the line, everybody stopped calling him Arthur and started calling the orange-haired boy "Soda Pop," on account of his love for fizzy, sugary drinks that turned good teeth bad.

"Whatchu guys up to?" Soda Pop asked.

"Treasure huntin'," Malik drawled. "You can come if you want."

Soda Pop scratched his round belly, thinking it over. He said, "Got nothing else to do." And he followed along.

Tiana skipped to the lead. The boys talked about baseball teams and how the All-Star Game didn't mean nothing anymore. "My dad says it ain't what it used to be," Soda Pop said.

Malik mused, "I can't think of anything that is."

"Take a look what I got," Soda Pop said. He pulled out a thick stack of baseball cards from his back pocket. The two boys paused there on the ragged sidewalk, dandelions popping up from the cracks, flipping through the cards and commenting on each one.

After a while, Malik lifted his head. He

looked up the street. He looked down the street. "Where'd she go to now?" he wondered aloud.

Soda Pop shrugged, unworried. "Off somewhere's, I suppose."

Malik peered down the road and there it stood in the distance, like a beaten fighter after fifteen rounds in the ring. *The old place.* A shivery feeling squeezed Malik's heart like a sponge. "Come on," he said, hurrying in the direction of the old place.

"Hold up," Soda Pop said. He had dropped his cards to the curb.

"Not waiting," Malik said. "Catch up if you want." Off he went, walking fast, half running, in the direction of the old place. He called as he went, "Tiana? Hey, Tee? You holler if you hear me! Tiana, I'm not fooling around."

There was no sign of his sister.

Malik walked the length of the block and now stood staring at the old place.

The dusty yard was overgrown with tall grass and untrimmed bushes. The door was locked shut, with slats of wood nailed across it. All the windows were boarded up. There was no easy way inside. Malik figured it was unlikely that Tiana had gotten herself in there. But his heart still had that squeezed-out feeling.

"Tiana!" he hollered. "You best not be inside that house."

Malik's nerves jumped like live wires on the street. An inner voice told him, *This is no place for a little girl. Find your sister right now.*

Pasty-faced Soda Pop pulled up, bent over and wheezing, short of breath. "Anybody"—pause, gasp—"ever told you"—pause, pant—"you walk too fast?"

"Let's check around back," Malik replied, all business.

"I ain't going back there," Soda Pop said. "Not for a bag of gummy worms, I wouldn't. You know what folks say. A widow lady went crazy in there, before we was born. They took her away, loony as a jaybird. Place is haunted. Nope, I'm not going back there."

"Suit yourself," Malik shrugged.

And he went off, careful not to pass too near the old place, still looking for his lost sister.

THE BOX

He found Tiana squatting in the dirt about fifty feet behind the house. The edges of her dress were dirty and soiled.

"Tee!" he called out. "You shouldn't be back here."

"I found something."

"Nevermind that, let's go," Malik said.

"For real," Tiana said. "Come see for yourself."

The girl held a short, thick stick. When

Malik stepped forward, he could see that she had scraped a gash about four inches deep into the earth. And sure enough, something was buried down there.

Malik got on his knees for closer study. "It looks like a piece of wood or—"

"It's a box," Tiana said.

Malik turned to look at her. "How would you know?"

Tiana shrugged and blew a wild strand of black hair from her eyes. "I just do."

"Soda Pop!" Malik shouted. "Best come back here right now." He waited, listening. He called again, "Tiana maybe found treasure."

That got him moving.

It took some digging, but the work went faster after Malik fetched a small hand shovel from home. Twenty minutes later, they unearthed an old wooden box about the size of a loaf of bread. There was a padlock on it.

The three children sat wilting under the sun, staring at the box.

"Why would anybody bury a box?" Malik asked.

"Locked shut, too," Soda Pop said. "Must be something valuable inside."

"It's been nailed closed, too," Malik said. "See here?" He pointed to the nail heads, two on each corner of the box.

Tiana grew quiet, her eyes shut. When she opened them, the little girl said, "She wants us to open it."

Soda Pop snorted, "What are you talking about, Tiana?"

Tiana blinked. There was a faraway look in her eyes. "Nothing," she answered. "I didn't mean nothing by it."

Malik held the box in his lap. He brushed off the last bits of dirt and clay, using his T-shirt to polish it clean. He turned the box over to study the bottom panel. Someone had carved into the wood.

TOUEMT ELOSW ONEVAH EBOTE SIM ORPI

"What's this mean, you think?"

He tried sounding out the words. "Touemt . . . elosw . . . onevah?"

"Sounds like French or something," Soda Pop figured.

Malik offered the box to Soda Pop for inspection, but the boy shook his head. "Nuh-unh, no way. I ain't touching it," he said. "That box gives me the heebie-jeebies."

"The heebie-jeebies? Why for?" Malik asked.

"Just a bad feeling I got," Soda Pop said. "Something about it makes me feel clammy inside. Like I just ate a bowl of ice cream too fast." He shivered.

Malik fingered the lock. "We could bust it open, I guess."

"Don't mess with it," Soda Pop warned.

"Why not?" Malik asked.

"It's not ours to bust open," Soda Pop replied. He looked up at the broken windows of the old place, the peeled paint. "I just don't think we should, that's all. We should leave it right here in the hole you dug."

"It's mine," Tiana said flatly. "I found it."

Malik appraised his sister. "I suppose so," he decided. "But how did you find it, Tiana? What were you doing back here in the first place?"

"I heard her calling me, '*Let me out! Let me out!*'" Tiana answered. "She promised to be good. So I came to the rescue."

CRUMMY OLD DOLL

Opening the box wasn't easy. Mr. Rice was busy snoozing at home. They grabbed tools from the garage: a lead pipe, a hammer, two screwdrivers, and a big axe. Malik suggested they retreat a distance from the house. "No sense waking Pa," he said. "He gets grumpy without his sleep."

Their skinny black cat, Midnight, followed the children from a distance. Just curious, Malik guessed, the way cats are born to be.

They reached a familiar clearing in the woods and set down the box. For a moment, the children all stood staring, as if the box was a magnet that pulled their eyeballs to it. No one spoke. "Might as well get it done," Malik muttered. He knelt down and tried to pry it open with the screwdriver.

"That ain't gonna work," Soda Pop observed.

Annoyed, Malik offered him the box. "You wanna try?"

Soda Pop stepped back quickly. He tripped on a root and fell on his backside. Tiana laughed, a little cruelly. Soda Pop wasn't hurt, so Malik let her get away with that unkindness without a scolding. Besides, it was kind of funny, the way he fell on his *boom, boom, boom*.

Malik grabbed the axe and felt its heft in his hands. "Better step back," he warned. He raised the axe high and let it fall.

THWACK, SMASH!

The box was well-built, but no match for a sharp axe. Bits of wood splintered loose and one corner of the box split open.

Midnight rubbed up against Malik's legs. He hissed and spat at the box, raising his back in an arch.

"Shhh, Midnight," Malik hushed. He smoothed the cat's raised fur. "What's gotten into you?"

Soda Pop stepped forward. "What's inside it?"

"Hold on a minute," Malik said. "Gimmie that hammer, Tee."

Working carefully, Malik pried apart the box.

"Is that all there is?" Soda Pop asked. "A crummy old doll?"

And in truth, that's all there was. Just an ordinary doll—and not a very fine one,

either. The doll had curly black hair with a red ribbon in it, a dirty blue-and-white–striped dress, and one of its eyes was missing entirely. The doll's painted face was badly cracked and worn.

"I don't get it." Soda Pop scratched his head, befuddled.

Malik pushed the doll aside. He searched through the scraps of wood. "There was nothing else in it," he said. There was disappointment in his voice.

Tiana picked up the doll and pressed it close to her chest. "I love it," she said. "I love it lots."

"Well, fine for you, I guess," Malik said. "At least you got a dolly out of it, but I was hoping for something more interesting."

"Yeah, like money," Soda Pop complained.

"She's better than money," Tiana said, examining the doll closely. "She's just about the best thing I've ever seen."

Soda Pop snorted, "What are you talking about, Tee? That's just a stupid old doll somebody buried in the ground. Ugliest thing I've ever seen, too."

Tiana clutched the doll tight to her chest. She glared at Soda Pop with a look of pure poison. "Don't talk. *You're* the ugly one," she said.

At that moment, a darkness fell over them. A gust of wind kicked up. The trees bent and swayed.

Malik looked up, wonderingly. "We better get going. Storm's coming."

But it was too late. Thunder cracked, lightning flashed. The clouds burst open and poured down buckets of rain. The three children were soaked to the bone by the time they got home.

VOICES IN THE DARK

For the next few days, the doll, now named Selena, went everywhere with Tiana. The two were inseparable. And for some reason, it got on Malik's nerves.

"Can't you put down that doll for one little minute?" he said.

Tiana pouted. "Selena's not hurting nobody."

Malik couldn't argue with that. But still, there was something about that doll he didn't like. Tiana lugged it around everywhere. She even brought the doll into bed with her!

One night, as he got ready for bed, Malik paused by Tiana's door. She should have been asleep half an hour ago. But Malik heard talking. Two voices. Was his mother in there? Malik didn't think so. He recognized Tiana's little girl voice, whispering softly. The other voice was scratchy.

"They called me ugly," the scratchy voice said.

"Shhh, that's all right," Tiana whispered.

Malik put an ear to the door.

"The fat one's a mean beast," the scratchy voice said. "I might hurt him. I will, I will. Call me ugly and you get hurt, you do."

"He's named Soda Pop," Tiana said.

"I'll get him, I will. You watch me, just watch. He'll cry soon enough," the voice threatened.

There was silence.

Finally, Tiana said, "I love you, Selena."

Malik had heard enough. He rapped on the door. "Who you talking to in there, Tee?"

"Shhhh," a voice whispered.

"Tee? Answer me."

A light turned off. The crack under the door went black.

"No one, just me," Tiana called.

Malik turned the knob. He pushed open the door. The light from the hallway leaked into the room. He saw his sister in bed, the covers tucked up to her chin. She blinked at him and smiled gently.

Gazing around the room, Malik spied the old doll on the shelf beside a few books and toys. Its one eye was closed.

Malik frowned. "Time for sleep, Tee. Stop your silly games."

Tiana stretched her arms. She yawned.

"Good night, Malik." She rolled on her side, turning her back to her brother.

"Okay, 'night." Malik began to pull the door shut. He paused. "You okay, Tee? Everything good?"

She didn't answer.

CLICK.

It was a faint sound, but Malik heard it loud and clear. **CLICK**. The sound of a doll's eye . . . opening.

Malik stole a glance at the doll. The hallway light fell across her, slicing like a sword of light through the darkness.

One eye missing. The other eye . . . open.

Strange. Its head was now turned directly at him. How could that be?

For the first time, Malik noticed there was a faint smile on its painted face. Like that famous painting, the Mona Lisa.

What are you smiling about? he wondered.

Malik shivered, and shut the door tight.

THE BOYS MAKE
A PLAN

Malik's mother sat at the sewing machine. She often made clothes for Tiana, little dresses and skirts. She was handy that way. Without so much as turning around, Mrs. Rice asked where in the world Malik was going with the cat dish.

"Just outside," he said.

"The cat eats inside," his mother said.

"Not lately," the boy explained.

The fact was, Midnight had lately refused to come indoors. Wouldn't step one paw into the house, no matter how hard Malik tried to coax it. "Come inside," he would say in his softest voice. "Here's your milk. I warmed it up for you, Midnight."

The skittish cat just backed away. It would rather starve than enter the house. Malik finally gave up. He began bringing food to the stoop out front. Midnight gobbled it up fast as lightning. Then the wild feline bolted into the woods.

Malik didn't know what to think. Could it be that Midnight had a girlfriend somewhere? Maybe he was spending time at some other house? But in Malik's mind he connected two things, the cat and the doll, linked by an invisible thread. He couldn't be sure, but Malik traced Midnight's strange behavior to the day they found the box behind the old place. He remembered the way Midnight arched his back. The way he hissed and spat in the woods.

The cat feared and hated the doll. But why?

It didn't make much sense.

But there it was. The plain truth. Malik wished he could talk to the cat. Ask questions. Get answers. He'd ask, "Hey, Midnight. What do you know about that old doll? Why don't you like it any?" Then maybe he'd softly confide into its whiskers, "Between us, I don't like it neither, not one bit. But I can't explain it. How about you?"

He called inside to his mother, "Maw, I'm going to Soda Pop's."

"Not so loud, Pa's sleeping," his mother called back. "You want to take Tiana with you?"

Malik paused. "Do I have to?"

"No," his mother said. "Not today, I guess you don't. She seems happy enough up in her room. Tiana and that doll. They have a special bond, those two, like peas in a pod. Don't be too long, Malik. I've got to get to work at the nursing home by lunch hour."

"Yes, Ma'am." The boy gave his mother a peck on the cheek. Then tramped his way to Soda Pop's house.

Soda Pop opened the door. His right hand was buried inside a big bag of potato chips. "Hey, Mal."

"Anybody home?"

"Just me," Soda Pop answered.

"You got a minute to talk?" Malik asked.

Soda Pop shrugged, looking around the empty house. "I got a lot of minutes. What's up?"

Malik plopped down on the living room couch. A small cloud of dust rose up and danced in the sunlit air. "I've been asking my-self questions all night. Why would anybody go to the trouble of putting a doll in a box? And locking it shut? Then nailing it tight to make double sure? And burying the box in the backyard? Triple sure that doll wouldn't get out. Huh, Soda Pop? Why would some-body go to all that trouble?"

Soda Pop chewed on his lip, then shrugged. Finally he said, "That's the million-dollar question, id'n it? I figure the crazy woman did it, before they hauled her away in a straight-jacket."

"Well, I got some ideas about how we can find the answer," Malik said.

"Yeah?"

"Two ideas, actually. First, we need to look at the writing on that box again. I think it might have been a code."

"I can study up on codes." Soda Pop

leaned forward, interested. "Get a book or something."

"Good. The other thing is, we need to find out more about the lady who used to live in that old place," Malik said.

"That was a long time ago," Soda Pop said. "Maybe we need to talk to somebody who is old. Real old. Like fifty and more."

Malik grinned. "I know a good place to start."

MALIK TAKES A TUMBLE

That night, Malik again waited outside Tiana's door, perfectly still. He tried not to move, not to breathe. It was full dark, past midnight. The house was quiet. The sleepers slept. Outside, wind pushed the leaves in the trees, the branches swayed and stretched their twisted fingers. The moon was pale, partly hidden by clouds. A thin black cat moved in the shadows, mewling.

Low, hushed voices spilled softly into the hallway. Malik listened closer. He could not make out the words. One voice whispered with a steady urgency. Tiana's voice answered back, saying again and again, "Yes, yes, I know. Yes, yes."

A chill ran through Malik. She was just six years old. A little girl. What was happening with his sister?

CREEEAAAK.

He stepped into the room.

Tiana was sitting up in her bed. The old doll was clutched close to her chest. Both heads stared at Malik with the same expression. A plastic emptiness. Tiana looked tired, worn out. There were dark circles under her eyes. One eye, Malik noticed, looked bloodshot. Swollen.

She wore a red ribbon in her hair, identical to the one worn by the doll. For a moment, the living girl and the doll appeared to Malik as Siamese twins. Connected somehow.

"You're still up," Malik said. "It's late, Tee."

Tiana shifted and the doll turned its head. It seemed to move itself closer to Tiana's ear.

Malik heard murmuring. He didn't like it and said so.

"We're just talking," Tiana said. She smiled, a Mona Lisa smile. Happiness, sadness, kindness, cruelty. Malik couldn't tell.

He came to the edge of the bed. "Well, it's bedtime now. Long past. Gimmie the doll."

Tiana pulled away. "No, it's mine!"

Malik snatched the doll from his sister's grip. "I said give it."

She fought him, but Tiana was no match for her older, stronger brother.

"I want her back!" Tiana cried. "I'm telling!!"

"Shhhh, you'll wake the dead," Malik scolded. "You'll get your doll back in the morning. I'm just putting it out in the hall. You need to behave, or I'll be the one who tells about your little secret."

The girl pouted. But after a moment, Tiana yawned and a bone-deep tiredness fell over her. In that instant, she once again became the sweet little girl that Malik had known all his life.

He tossed the doll into the corner of the hallway. Malik stepped into the bathroom. He washed his hands and face. He stared at himself in the mirror. The face he saw was full of worry. Something was not right. He felt it. Something about that doll wasn't right.

Malik turned off the light and stepped into

the hall. He noticed the glitter of a coin on the floor by the top of the stairs. He bent for it.

The boy did not hear the door to his sister's room open. Nor did he notice the soft, swift, shuffling footfalls on the floor.

He felt a push—as if two small hands pressed hard against his back—and Malik was suddenly off-balance, falling, tumbling through the dark, bumping and twisting down the hard wooden stairs.

It was a wonder he didn't break his neck.

A wonder he did not die.

When his mother, awakened by the clatter, came rushing, she found Malik at the bottom of the stairs. His forehead was bloodied. His eyes were glazed. She fussed over her son, examining his arms and legs, feeling for broken bones. "What happened?" she asked.

Malik gazed up the stairs.

He thought he heard the light scampering of little feet.

There was no one there.

Not his sister.

Not the doll.

"Just tripped, I guess," he murmured. "Stupid me."

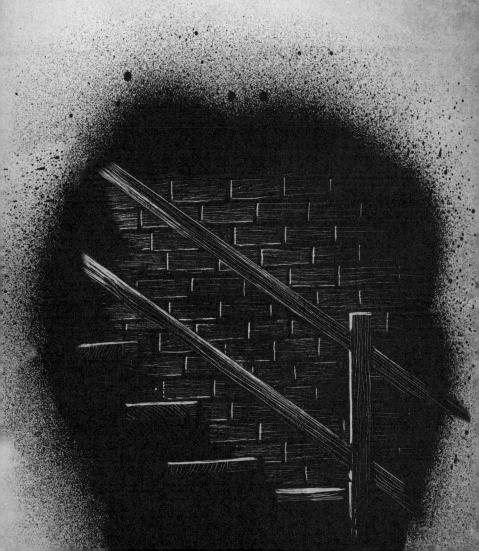

TWINS

D o you like it?"

Tiana was pleased. She stood in her pretty new dress. A real smile on her face. Another glimpse of what she used to be like.

"I asked Mama to make it for me," she said.

Malik dug his hands into his pockets. His eyes moved from his sister to the doll in her arms. Their dresses were now identical. Blue-and-white striped. Both girl and doll wore a red ribbon in their hair.

"What's wrong with your eye?" he asked. "It's half closed."

Tiana shrugged. "Mama says it might be pink eye. Or maybe I got a spider bite. Now I look like Selena. Don't you think?"

She smiled a Mona Lisa smile.

"I guess you do. How about you leave that doll at home for once?" Malik suggested. "Come outside with me. We could shoot baskets. Play horse. Or we could pack a picnic, go fishing by the river. What do you think, Selena? I mean, Tiana!"

Malik caught the error immediately. It was a simple mistake, calling his sister by the doll's name. But it haunted him just the same.

"Selena doesn't like those things," Tiana replied. "She says they're dumb."

Malik's mood darkened. "Suit yourself." He wheeled and made for the front door. "I've got something to do, Tee. I'll be back in one hour. Okay? One hour. You and that doll sit around all you want. Just don't leave the house, you hear? Daddy's home. If you need something, just wake him. But if I was you, I'd wait unless it's a real emergency."

Tiana didn't answer.

She was already gone.

Up in her room, Malik guessed.

He thought of his mother's words, *"They have a special bond."*

Tiana and that doll.

They were becoming more alike every day.

His head felt like it was on fire. His stomach was in knots. He knew he shouldn't leave his sister alone. Not even for an hour. But this was important. He had things to figure out. And he was scared.

For the first time, he was really scared.

Malik burst through the front door,

leaped down the porch steps, and raced into the woods. He found the shattered, wooden pieces from the box where they'd been left in the clearing. One piece was of special interest. He tucked the plank under his arm and went to find Soda Pop.

The two boys sat on the curb, staring at the message.

TOUEMT ELOSW ONEVAH EBOTE SIM ORPI

Soda Pop leafed through the pages of the book he gotten earlier that day from the library, *Secret Codes and Messages*. He may have been a junk-food junkie, but Soda Pop could be pretty sharp sometimes.

This was one of those times.

Malik kept trying to sound out the words. "Onevah . . . ebo . . . tay . . . sim . . ."

"Wait a sec," Soda Pop said. "It talks in here about reverse codes and mirror codes. Let's try reading it backwards."

He scribbled in a notebook:

IPRO MIS ETOBE HAVENO WSOLE TMEOUT

"Okay," Malik said. "I can see some words in there: *To. Be. Have. No. So. Me. Out*."

"I," said Soda Pop.

"What?"

"*I*, that's the first word in the message," Soda Pop answered. He flipped through the book and paused on a page, scanning the words. "This could also be a Space Code. They put the spaces in the wrong places to mess us up," he said. "Let's mush 'em together."

IPROMISETOBEHAVENOWSOLETMEOUT

After a few minutes, Malik got it. Almost. "I promise to be . . . have now so . . . let me out."

"It's one word," Soda Pop said. "Behave." He jotted down the message one final time.

I PROMISE TO BEHAVE. SO NOW LET ME OUT.

"The doll wrote it!" Malik said.

"Wait, what?" Soda Pop asked.

"It's alive!" Malik said. "Don't you see? That's why the letters were backwards—she wrote it from *inside* the box. She was asking to be let out!"

I PROMISE
TO BEHAVE.
SO NOW LET
ME OUT.

MALIK IN THE NURSING HOME

It was a quick bike ride to the nursing home—if you pedaled like your hair was on fire.

Malik made it in six minutes flat.

His mother had worked in the kitchen since he was a baby. Malik was a familiar face to the nurses on staff. When he was little, before he could fend for himself, Malik spent a lot of time in the back rooms. Drawing pictures, building with Legos, eating snacks, looking at picture books. It was cheaper than hiring a babysitter.

The home was a curious world, full of odd smells and old people. Most folks were frail, like glass figurines on a shelf you shouldn't touch for fear they might break. Some still had sharp minds. They played cards, watched tv, and carried on conversations. Then there were the folks who seemed . . . finished. Like burnt-down candles. When Malik walked the halls, he would sometimes glimpse them sitting in their rooms. Alone and silent, waiting for a bus that would never come.

It was sad, and Malik tried not to think about it.

"Say, Malik! What are you doing here today?" Curtis the custodian chirped. He stopped pushing a mop around the floor and, instead, leaned on it with both hands. Happy to pause and chat.

"Just thought I'd stop by," Malik said.

"Getting big!" Curtis observed. "If I don't watch out, you'll be taking my job."

No, thanks, Malik thought. He had bigger dreams. But he said with a grin, "I just might."

He started to walk away, then thought twice. "You've been here a long time, right?"

Curtis looked up, as if the answer was written on the ceiling. "Twenty years, next September."

Malik whistled. He decided to take a shot. "You remember the old place on my block. Right? The one nobody lives in."

The brightness left the custodian's eyes. "I know it," he said. "That place is bad business. Bad voodoo over there."

"Do you know anything about . . ." Malik said, stepping forward. "I mean, can you tell me about it?"

"That's not my place to say," Curtis said.

"It's important," Malik said. "It means a lot to me. Please."

Maybe the old man was in a talkative mood that day. Maybe there was something about the way Malik asked. The look in his eyes.

"There's a patient here," Curtis said. "Miss Delgado. She was the last person who lived there—but that was, oh, thirty-something years ago. She used to be in the mental hospital, you know, the asylum. But she's no trouble anymore."

"She's here?" Malik asked.

"Room 17, just down the hall," Curtis said. "I don't think she can help you, Malik. She hasn't said ten words in all the time she's been here."

"Can I see her?" Malik asked.

Curtis looked up and down the empty hall. "She's been through enough. Leave an old woman alone."

"Please, I'll be respectful," Malik said. "Just for a minute?"

"If you get caught," Curtis said with a sigh, "I don't know anything about it. Understand?"

He turned in the opposite direction from Room 17 and pushed the mop down the hall. The conversation was over. Malik was on his own.

THE GRAY-HAIRED
LADY AT THE WINDOW

The old woman sat by the window. Her hands were in her lap. She never moved. She scarcely breathed.

Her eyes stared at some point in the distance, but at the same time, it looked to Malik like they weren't focused on anything at all. She looked, but she did not see.

Her hair was wild and uncombed and completely gray. There was a red ribbon in it. The same as Selena. The same as Tiana.

Malik gulped. He shuffled closer.

The old woman did not turn to look at him. She was all alone in the world. Someone had gone to the trouble of putting makeup on her face. It was caked on thick, and it cracked along the wrinkles. Red lipstick was smeared across her mouth.

There was a black patch over one eye.

Malik coughed, drawing closer.

The woman did not stir.

"Miss?" Malik whispered softly. "Excuse me, Miss?"

There was no response.

Malik glanced to the door and the hallway outside. He didn't have much time.

He began talking:

"My name is Malik Rice. I live a few houses down from where you used to live, back in the old days. Well, see, my sister and me—her name is Tiana, she's a beautiful girl, just six years this April—well, we took something from your yard. And maybe we shouldn't have taken it."

He paused, watching for some sign from the woman.

"We found a box," he said. "There was a doll inside it."

CLICK. Malik watched the woman's one eye blink.

Slowly, slowly, the old woman turned to look at Malik. Even so, it was as if she were gazing past him, staring at some other horror. The bony fingers of her hands grabbed Malik's arm. She squeezed, digging sharp nails into his skin. Malik moved to pull away, but she only squeezed tighter. Gripped by some unknown terror.

She spoke in a dry, brittle whisper. "The one-eyed witch . . . fear, fear . . . the one-eyed witch."

Malik jerked away hard to escape the old woman's grip. Drops of blood formed on his skin. Her trembling hands came up to the side of her face. Her mouth opened wide as if to scream. But no sound issued from her lips.

The scream was silent.

Her body began to shake.

This had been a mistake, a terrible mistake. Malik backed away, shuffling toward the door. "What does she want?" he asked. Desperate for an answer. "The one-eyed witch! What does the witch want?"

CLICK. The woman blinked again.

Her mouth contorted into a twisted grimace. The woman's voice sounded like dead leaves in November, crackling on the sidewalk. "What the witch wants," the gray-haired woman said, "what the witch wants . . . is to become . . . a real girl."

THE FIGHT

"I'm back," Malik called as he entered the house. Silence. He walked to the bottom of the stairs. "Tee? You up there?"

No answer.

He checked the bedroom. No Tiana. No one-eyed doll. Moving swiftly, he searched every corner of the small house. Calling softly, afraid to wake his father. "Tiana? Tee? Answer me."

Nothing.

He was frantic now, his body tingling. Where was she? Where could they have gone?

And he knew. Right at that moment. He knew.

The old place.

Tiana had taken the doll back to the old place. Or perhaps, the witch had taken Tiana.

His little sister. Just six years old.

It was Malik's job to look after her. To take care of her, no matter what.

He ran without touching the ground, his heart in his throat.

In two leaps, Malik landed on the front porch on the old place. The wood splintered under his feet. The door was ajar. Malik entered.

"Tiana!" he called.

A chill ran through his body.

The house was cold. A cloud of smoke

came from his mouth like on a winter's day. Malik shivered. He stepped fully inside.

CLICK.

He sensed it. The witch was in the house, somewhere. The rooms were dank and empty, dusty and dark. Tiana was here, too. He could feel it in his bones.

Malik crept deeper past the entranceway, deeper into the darkness. He did not see a black shape slink into the house behind him. Its paws made no sound.

Tiana was on the floor in the living room. She lay sprawled on her back, legs spread, arms wide at each side, as if she were about to make a snow angel. The little girl stared vacantly at the ceiling. He felt her skin. Tiana was cold, so cold. Her felt for her heart.

It was beating. She was alive.

"Tiana, can you hear me?"

A rustle came from behind him.

He spun around to see the one-eyed witch. Standing upright. She moved quickly, mouth wicked, teeth sharp.

MEEEEOOOOOORRRRWWW!

Out of the darknness, Midnight pounced on the witch. Claws slashed, howls erupted. Sounds of biting and screeching and wild cries filled the room.

Malik crouched beside his sister, frozen in fear. He watched the fierce battle. Suddenly, Midnight was thrown against the wall. The cat tried to rise, but could not. One of its back legs gave out. There was blood smeared on the wall. The witch cackled in triumph.

That's when Malik saw it.

A brick.

A red brick on the floor.

Without thought, Malik's hand reached

out. His fingers curled around it. He raised the brick up, and down it fell, down upon the head of the one-eyed witch.

The witch slumped to the floor.

Its one eye shut.

12

MALIK'S LONG WALK

For Malik, the rest was a blur.

He carried his sister home. She was cold. Limp in his arms. He kissed her, talked to her, squeezed her tight. Tiana did not respond.

Up the stairs they went. He tucked her into bed, piled the blankets warm around her.

He raced back to the old place, ready for battle. But the one-eyed witch still lay on the floor. *Dead*, he thought. Malik looked around for Midnight, but the tough, old cat was gone.

It must have limped off into the woods. He carried the doll back home, then dumped it in an empty garbage can at the side of his house. Malik found thick rope and tied the lid shut, just in case. He tightened the rope. Tied a knot, then another, then another.

Next, he called his mother. Woke his father. Told them that Tiana was sick. She needed a doctor. And soon the doctor came. She was a tall, graceful woman dressed in a white lab coat. Dr. Owens. She sat at the side of the bed to examine his sister. And after a while, the doctor came out. "We'll let her rest for now," the doctor said. "She needs sleep. Perhaps tomorrow . . ."

Her voice trailed off.

She spoke quietly with Malik's parents in the next room. He heard his mother sob. His father tried to comfort her, saying, "There, there. There, there."

Malik awoke that night to noises in the yard.

Bumps in the night.

THUMP, THUMP, THUMP.
THUMP,
THUMP,
THUMP!

The one-eyed witch was awake.

Malik sat up. Got dressed. Tied his laces.

He had one last job to do.

He took a hammer from the shed and grabbed his school backpack. The witch did not wish to come. She fought him. But the hammer convinced her.

Malik walked the roads by himself that starry night, dimly lit by a sickle moon. The pack was slung over his shoulder. He gripped the hammer in his hand.

All the while, the one-eyed witch whispered from inside the pack. Pleaded with him. Promised to behave. Begged for kindness, asked for mercy.

The witch cried, "Oh, dear boy, sweet boy, gentle child. You do not wish to harm me. I am sorry, a thousand times sorry! Search your heart! Forgive poor me, little me."

Malik trudged on, tramping through the warm night. Finally, he stopped on a footbridge that spanned a great and raging river.

"Do you hear that, witch?" he said.

"No, no, no!" cried the one-eyed witch. "Water, I will drown. You can't! Mercy. I beg you, mercy! You nasty beast! You horrible, nasty, evil beast—"

Malik pulled the doll from his backpack. The hastily tied rope had loosened around her, and fell away. Malik was resolute. He dropped the witch into the night. It fell and fell until, *splash*, the doll hit the water and disappeared from sight.

The next morning, Tiana awoke. She appeared refreshed, happy. Mrs. Rice hummed and fixed breakfast. Malik's father stayed home from work. Malik stole a moment alone with Tiana. "She's gone now," he whispered. "I got rid of her forever."

Tiana looked puzzled. "What are you talking about?"

Malik paused, uncertain. "The doll. Selena."

Tiana smiled. "You know I don't play with dolls, silly. I like hula hoops and basketballs, rainbows and lollipops, and frogs in muddy creeks!"

She laughed, and Malik laughed with her.

He understood at last. She didn't remember. It was all forgotten, like a bad dream that disappears in the warm light of morning.

A nightmare, unremembered.

MEOW, MEOW!

Midnight was at the screen door. "Look, he's back!" Malik cried.

"He's been fighting," Tiana noticed. "Look at his ear." A hunk of the cat's left ear was missing, as if it had been bitten off.

Malik opened the door. The cat hesitated at the threshold, sniffing the air. Midnight stepped inside, limping a bit, and rubbed against Tiana's legs. The girl scooped him up and squeezed him tight. "It looks like you need some extra loving," Tiana said.

And Midnight purred.

THE GIRL BY THE RIVER

A small, blonde-haired girl hummed happily by the banks of the river. It was a glorious morning, full of sunshine and white, puffy clouds. She had tented in a nearby campsite with her parents. Now they took a pleasant morning walk, turning toward the river to romp and splash in the cool water.

"Look, Mama!" the girl cried. "Look what I found!"

She fished a wet doll out of the water, where it had been caught on the branch of a bush. The doll had soggy black hair with a red ribbon in it. Her dress was ruined, though the girl could see it had once been pretty. Blue-and-white striped. One of the doll's eyes was missing entirely. Its face was cracked and worn.

"Can I keep it? Can I?" the girl asked.

"No, that's disgusting," her father said. "It's covered with germs. Leave that here. We'll get you a new doll another time."

The girl looked to her mother. "Mom? Please? We can clean it up, can't we?"

The mother glanced at her husband. She shrugged. "Sure, why not? I might even make her a new dress," she offered.

"Oh, thank you!" the girl said. She hugged the doll tight to her chest. "I love it. I love it so much!"

Round and round it goes. The one-eyed witch. Trapped in the body of a doll. Gets passed from hand to hand.

She wants to be real again.

To walk and talk like a girl again.

Look around. Are there any old dolls in your house? Do its eyes click when they open? Perhaps it's time to find a box. And dig a hole. And hope that no one ever, ever digs it up.

Some things are better left buried.

LOOKING FOR MORE
THRILLS AND CHILLS?

DON'T MISS THE SIXTH

SCARY TALES

BOOK . . .

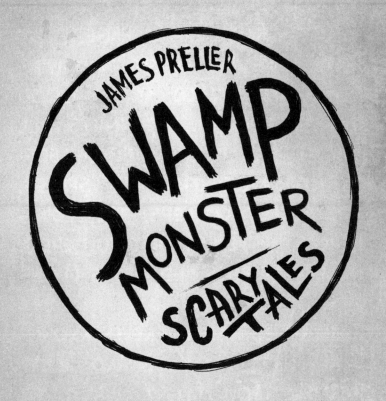

JAMES PRELLER

SWAMP MONSTER

SCARY TALES

Illustrated by IACOPO BRUNO

BEFORE YOU TURN THE PAGE, FIRST MAKE SURE THE DOORS AND WINDOWS ARE LOCKED. IT'S A GOOD IDEA TO TURN ON THE LIGHTS. ALL THE LIGHTS. IN EVERY ROOM. BETTER TO AVOID THE DARK SPACES. THE SECRET CORNERS. THE HIDING PLACES. WE ADVISE THAT YOU CHECK UNDER THE BEDS AND IN THE CLOSETS.

BECAUSE, HEY, YOU NEVER KNOW.

ALL SETTLED? SNUG AND COZY? TERRIFIC. YOU MIGHT WANT TO IGNORE THE SCRATCHING AT THE WINDOW. IT'S ONLY THE WIND. NO WORRIES, IT'S JUST THE WIND. . . .

PLUNK, SPLAT, GLORP...

The Dirge Chemical Plant had been dumping toxic sludge into the swamp for the past twenty-five years.

The illegal dumping was a fact well-known to the folks in Avarice County, but no one complained.

Most of the waste leaked into remote swampland and drained into the good earth. Besides, Dirge Chemical was owned by the wealthiest family in the state. It employed more than five hundred hardworking men and women from all over the county. Folks depended on that plant for their families' survival. If it were shut down, they'd lose their jobs and their homes. And what then?

So when it came to a little bit of poison sludge dripping into the ground, folks looked the other way.

Drip, drop, splurk. It leaked into the streams and waterways, into ponds and lakes. It soaked deep into the ground.

What about the creatures that lived in that environment? The fish and birds and snakes and gators? The animals that drank the water daily? That swam amid the burbling poisons? Well, most died off. But some adapted. Mutated. Learned how to feed off the toxic waste. Those few creatures grew stronger, bigger, tougher.

More dangerous, too.

The pollution was worst in Dismal Swamp, deep in the wooded wilderness. Hardly anybody lived out there. Nobody important. Some poor folks, mostly. And that's where our story begins—with two boys, Lance and Chance LaRue. On this day, they were knee-deep in the foul, nasty water, swiping at mosquitoes, searching for frogs.

That was their first mistake.

SWAMP PET

Chance and Lance were brothers, and twins. They both had narrow faces, pointy noses, large eyes, and long yellow hair that had never seen a comb. Chance and Lance even shared each other's clothes half the time, inside-out and *still* muddy.

Chance was the first one born, the oldest by three minutes, and still in a hurry. Lance was the twin with a chipped front tooth and worried eyes. That's how folks told them apart.

"Chance is the lively one," his mother would say. "Lance always looks like he thinks a piano is about to fall on his head. Hasn't happened yet, though, and I'm mighty glad of that. Them pianos are expensive to repair."

Then she'd laugh and laugh, holding her round belly.

It was true. Lance was prone to accidents. He was the one who spilled milk, got splinters, sat in poison ivy, and got stung by bees. If Lance stood next to Chance in a thunderstorm, Lance would surely be the one who was struck by lightning. Chance wouldn't even so much as get wet.

Even so, despite these differences—or perhaps because of them—the two brothers loved each other fiercely. Maybe it was the hard times that kept the boys together. They both felt that same hunger in their bellies. Life was not easy at home. They were dirt poor and lived in a broken-down trailer behind

Dismal Swamp. Their daddy put it up on cinder blocks and there it remained, sagging into the mud, drained of color by the hot, Texas sun. Home, sweet home. Even worse, their daddy had a bad habit of disappearing for long stretches of time. Out hunting, or away with friends, or in locked up in the jail somewhere. Mama said he was a "ne'er-do-well." Chance and Lance didn't know what that meant, exactly, but they figured it was another way of saying "good-for-nothing."

Sad, but true.

On this sweltering summer morning, the boys headed deep into the shaded swampland. Chance carried a metal bucket in hopes they might capture some critter worth keeping. That was a constant pursuit for the boys: They longed for a pet. Once, the twins found a stray dog, and begged their mother to keep it. She replied, "Boys, I can barely feed you two. Ain't no way we can take in another hungry mouth," and that was that. No dog. End of discussion.

A muddy path skirted the edge of the swampy water. Fortified by peanut butter sandwiches, the boys felt unusually strong and adventurous. They went deeper into the woods than ever before. The trees thickened around them. Long limbs hung low. Spanish moss dangled from the branches like exotic drapes. Snakes slithered. Once in a while, a bird called. Not a song, so much as a warning.

Stay away, stay away.

The farther the boys traveled, the darker it got.

Lance stopped, slapped a mosquito on the back of his neck. The bug exploded, leaving behind a splash of blood. "I don't know, Chance," he said doubtfully. "Getting dark, getting late."

Chance chewed on a small stick. He spat out a piece of bark. "Let's keep on pushing ahead." And off he went, leading the way, content that Lance would surely follow.

After another while, Chance paused and stooped low, bringing his eyes close to the earth. He pointed to a track in the mud. "What you think, Lance?"

"Too big to be a gator," Lance said. He turned to peer into the dark, snake-infested water. "But I'd say it's gator-ish."

"Real big," Chance noted. "Heavy, too. You can tell 'cause the print sank way down."

"Guess you're right," Lance almost agreed.

"Here's another," Chance said, moving two steps to his right. "Three toes, webbed feet. Weird."

"Never seen the like of it before," Lance said. "Looks like it was moving fast, judging by the length of the stride—"

"—and headed right there," Chance said, pointing to the swamp, "into the water."

"You reckon those tracks were made by Bigfoot?" Lance asked.

Chance grinned at his brother. They both laughed and laughed, until the swamp swallowed up the sound. They stood together in eerie silence.

"Maybe we should head back," Lance suggested.

"I guess," Chance said, a little mournfully. "Hold on a minute. Is that an egg?"

He pointed to a hollow by the edge of the water.

"Good eyes, Chance. Turtle egg maybe," Lance confirmed.

Chance inspected it. Cocked his head, listened, looked around. No creature stirred.

"Let's take it home with us," he said.

"It don't feel right," Lance said.

"It'll be fine," Chance said. "You and me, we'll be real good mamas to this little baby."

Lance laughed. "I'm not no mama—that's your job. I'll be the papa."

And that was that. Chance made a bed of mud, twigs, and leaves in the bottom of the bucket. He gently lifted the egg and placed it inside.

"Carry that real soft," Lance joked. "Like a sweet, nice mama."

The boys turned back and headed home, stealing away with their curious prize.

Thank you for reading this FEIWEL AND FRIENDS book.
The Friends who made

SCARY TALES

possible are:

JEAN FEIWEL
publisher

LIZ SZABLA
editor in chief

RICH DEAS
senior creative director

HOLLY WEST
associate editor

DAVE BARRETT
executive managing editor

NICOLE LIEBOWITZ MOULAISON
production manager

LAUREN A. BURNIAC
editor

ANNA ROBERTO
associate editor

CHRISTINE BARCELLONA
administrative assistant

Follow us on Facebook or visit us
online at scarytalesbooks.com.

OUR BOOKS ARE FRIENDS FOR LI